The
Snowman
Raymond Briggs

PUFFIN

Other books
by Raymond Briggs

FATHER CHRISTMAS
FATHER CHRISTMAS GOES ON HOLIDAY
JIM AND THE BEANSTALK
FUNGUS THE BOGEYMAN

Based on Raymond Briggs' original story

THE SNOWMAN AND THE SNOWDOG BOOK AND CD

PUFFIN BOOKS
UK | USA | Canada | Ireland | Australia
India | New Zealand | South Africa
Puffin Books is part of the Penguin Random House group of companies
whose addresses can be found at global.penguinrandomhouse.com.

www.penguin.co.uk   www.puffin.co.uk   www.ladybird.co.uk

First published by Hamish Hamilton 1978
Published by Puffin Books 1980
Reissued 2018
003

Text and illustrations copyright © Raymond Briggs, 1978
Made and printed in China

ISBN: 978–0–141–37100–9

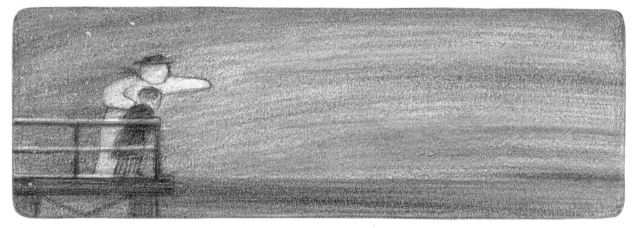

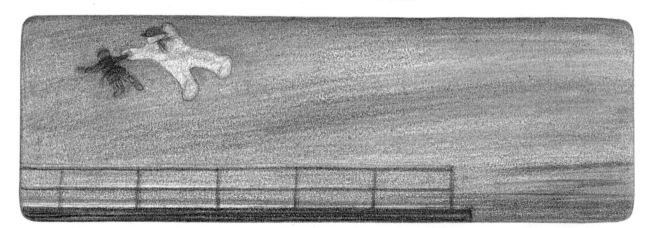

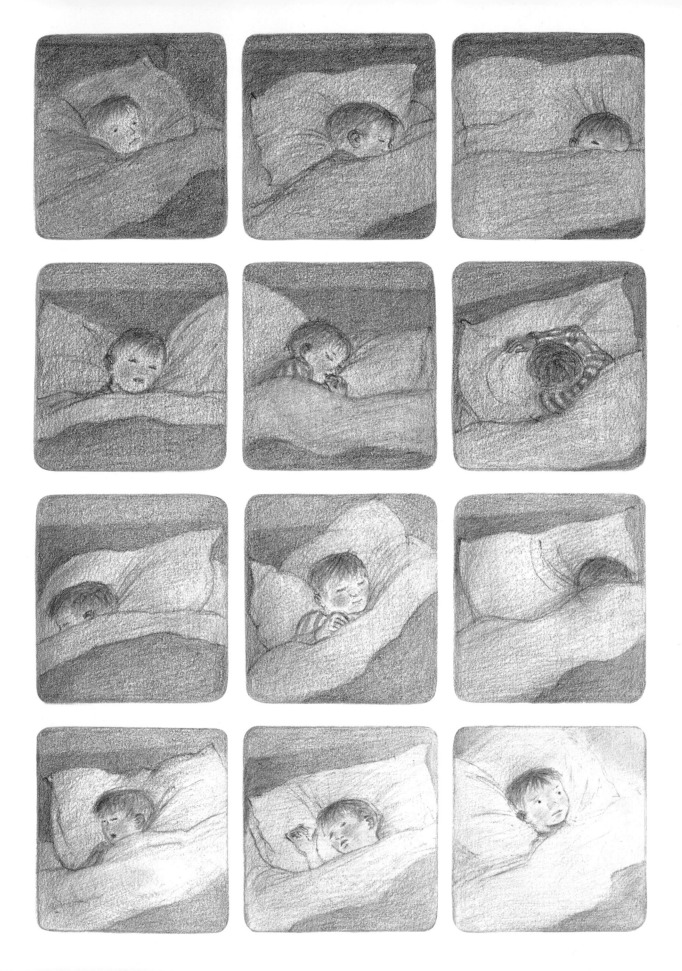